THE DIFFERENT Mommies AND Daddies

PAGE PUBLISHING, INC.
Conneaut Lake, PA

First originally published by Page Publishing 2022

ISBN 978-1-6624-5773-9 (hc)
ISBN 978-1-6624-5774-6 (digital)

Printed in the United States of America

THE
DIFFERENT
Mommies
AND
Daddies

Cavin Ramrup

GREEN PARK

1

All around the world, children have something that many shouldn't take for granted.
It is people who love and care for you. They can come in many forms, but we call them parents.

Many children will have parents from different parts of the world with unique beliefs and cultures. Their parents could have exciting careers as doctors, golfers, police officers, or even a famous art sculptor.

Many children will have parents that speak
different languages that you may not understand.
Their family will eat different foods
and have unfamiliar accents that they
learned to do from their native land.

Some parents could be grandmas and grandpas
who raise you to strive for the best.
Some parents could be uncles and aunts that
want to see you grow in life and progress.

Some children may have one mommy and one
daddy who love them with all their heart.
Some children may have two mommies
or two daddies. Don't be confused; they
love you all the same from the start.

Many children may not have parents right
from the start, but people will come into
their life to provide love and joy.
It could be gentle strangers who
raise you to become strong, kind,
and loving little girls and boys.

12

Some children may have one parent who plays
the role of both a mom and a dad.
They're like superheroes, with superabilities; they'll
be there to cheer you up when you're sad.

Some children have parents who are away for a while to perform different duties and tasks. Just remember, they love you and are excited to hear about your day; that will be the first thing they ask.

Life will be hard and confusing at times, but remember
to stay positive and try not to be sad or to pout.
You have parents who love and will guide
you to never give up or drop out.

Throughout life, remember to give it
your all and try your best.
Your parents are here to support you to overcome
any difficult challenge, obstacle, or test.

As you grow up, you will meet many friends from different backgrounds and ethnicities.
They could live in small rural farm towns or suburbs or places with tall buildings in big cities.

Remember children, when you grow up and meet friends with different parents from around the world. Remember to be kind, understanding and caring and you will grow up to be respectful boys and girls.

ABOUT THE AUTHOR

Cavin Ramrup is a seasoned professional in the finance world. His passions lie in real estate, boating, and spending time with his family. Forever the entrepreneur, after the birth of his daughter, he became committed to creating relatable content in children's books. During bedtime rituals, Cavin would find himself making up stories to help his daughter feel more comfortable in her day-to-day activities. As a Jersey City native, he is passionate about creating content for diversity and inclusion.

CPSIA information can be obtained
at www.ICGtesting.com
Printed in the USA
BVHW020958010322
630220BV00021B/285